The Wisdom of the East Series

东方智慧丛书

Editors-in-Chief: Tang Wenhui   Liu Zhiqiang

主编：汤文辉   刘志强

Academic Adviser: Zhang Baoquan

学术顾问：张葆全

Chinese-English

汉 英 对 照

Standards for Being a Good Student and Child

———————— • ————————

弟 子 规

Written by（Qing Dynasty）Li Yuxiu   Jia Cunren

原著：（清）李毓秀   贾存仁

Commented by Fan Huajie

释析：樊华杰

Proofread by Zhang Baoquan

中文审读：张葆全

Translated by Shen Fei

翻译：沈菲

Illustrated by Yin Hong   Guan Ruilin   Lai Junfei   Yang Yang

绘图：尹红   关瑞琳   赖俊妃   杨阳

· 桂林 Gui Lin ·

GUANGXI NORMAL UNIVERSITY PRESS
广西师范大学出版社

图书在版编目（CIP）数据

弟子规：汉英对照 / 樊华杰释析；沈菲译；尹红等绘.
桂林：广西师范大学出版社，2016.5（2017.5 重印）
（东方智慧丛书 / 汤文辉等主编）
ISBN 978-7-5495-7977-8

Ⅰ. ①弟… Ⅱ. ①樊…②沈…③尹… Ⅲ. ①古汉语—
启蒙读物—汉、英 Ⅳ. ①H194.1

中国版本图书馆 CIP 数据核字（2016）第 057783 号

广西师范大学出版社出版发行

（ 广西桂林市中华路 22 号 邮政编码：541001 ）
网址：http://www.bbtpress.com
出版人：张艺兵
全国新华书店经销
桂林广大印务有限责任公司印刷
（ 桂林市临桂县秧塘工业园西城大道北侧广西师范大学出版社集团
有限公司创意产业园 邮政编码：541100 ）
开本：880 mm × 1 240 mm 1/32
印张：6.875 字数：104 千字 图：89 幅
2016 年 5 月第 1 版 2017 年 5 月第 2 次印刷
定价：68.00 元

如发现印装质量问题，影响阅读，请与印刷厂联系调换。

总　序

　　文化交流对人类社会的存在与发展至关重要。季羡林先生曾指出，文化交流是推动人类社会前进的主要动力之一，文化一旦产生，就必然交流，这种交流是任何力量也阻挡不住的。由于文化交流，世界各民族的文化才能互相补充，共同发展，才能形成今天世界上万紫千红的文化繁荣现象。[1]

　　中国与东盟国家的文化交流亦然，并且具有得天独厚的优势。首先，中国与东盟许多国家地理相接，山水相连，不少民族之间普遍存在着跨居、通婚现象，这为文化交流奠定了良好的地理与人文基础。其次，古代中国与世界其他国家建立起的"海上丝绸之路"为中国与东盟国家的经济、文化交流创造了有利的交通条件。

　　中国与东盟诸多使用不同语言文字的民族进行思想与文化对话，自然离不开翻译。翻译活动一般又分为口译和笔译两类。有史记载的

---

[1]季羡林：《文化的冲突与融合·序》，载张岱年、汤一介等《文化的冲突与融合》，北京
　　大学出版社，1997年，第2页。

中国与东盟之间的口译活动可以追溯至西周时期，但笔译活动则出现在明代，至今已逾五百年的历史。

在过去五百年的历史长河中，东盟国家大量地译介了中国的文化作品，其中不少已经融入到本国的文化中去。中国译介东盟国家的作品也不在少数。以文字为载体的相互译介活动，更利于文化的传承与发展，把中国与东盟国家的文化交流推上了更高的层次。

2013年9月，国务院总理李克强在广西南宁举行的第十届中国—东盟博览会开幕式上发表主旨演讲时指出，中国与东盟携手开创了合作的"黄金十年"。他呼吁中国与东盟百尺竿头更进一步，创造新的"钻石十年"。2013年10月，习近平总书记在周边外交工作座谈会上强调要对外介绍好我国的内外方针政策，讲好中国故事，传播好中国声音，把中国梦同周边各国人民过上美好生活的愿望、同地区发展前景对接起来，让命运共同体意识在周边国家落地生根。于是，把中华文化的经典译介至东盟国家，不仅具有重要的历史意义，同时还蕴含着浓厚的时代气息。

所谓交流，自然包括"迎来送往"，《礼记》有言："往而不来，非礼也；来而不往，亦非礼也。"中国与东盟国家一样，既翻译和引进外国的优秀文化，同时也把本国文化的精髓部分推介出去。作为中国最具人文思想的出版社之一——广西师范大学出版社构想了《东方智慧丛书》，并付诸实践，不仅是中国翻译学界、人文学界的大事，更是中国与东盟进行良好沟通、增进相互了解的必然选择。广东外语外贸大学和广西民族大学作为翻译工作的主要承担方，都是国家外语非通用语种本科人才培养基地，拥有东盟语言文字的翻译优势。三个单位的合作将能够擦出更多的火花，向东盟国家更好地传播中华文化。

联合国教科文组织的官员认为，"文化交流是新的全球化现象"。[1]
我们希望顺应这一历史潮流与时代趋势，做一点力所能及的事。

是为序。

刘志强

2015 年 1 月 25 日

---

[1]《联合国教科文组织文化政策与跨文化对话司司长卡特瑞娜·斯泰诺的致辞》，载《世界文化的东亚视角》，北京大学出版社，2004年，第3页。

Preface to the Wisdom of the East Series

Cultural exchanges are of significant importance to the existence and development of human society. Mr. Ji Xianlin once pointed out that cultural exchange was one of the major driving forces for the progress of human society. It is inevitable that communications and exchanges will occur among different cultures. As a result, the interaction and mutual enrichment of cultures contribute to the formation of a diversified world featured by cultural prosperity.[1]

The cultural exchange between China and ASEAN countries, in the trend of mutual communication and interaction, also boasts of its own unique strengths. First of all, China borders many ASEAN countries both by land and by sea, and intermarriage and transnational settlement are common, all of which lay a solid foundation for cultural exchanges. In addition, the "Maritime Silk

[1] Ji Xianlin, "Preface to Cultural Conflicts and Integration", in *Cultural Conflicts and Integration*, edited by Zhang Dainian, Tang Yijie, et al. Beijing: Beijing University Press, 1997, p.2.

Road" developed by ancient China and other countries has helped pave the way to a smooth economic and cultural exchange between China and ASEAN countries.

People from China and ASEAN countries use different languages. Thus, to conduct a successful dialogue in the cultural field requires the involvement of translation and oral interpretation. Historical records show that the oral interpretation among people of China and ASEAN can be dated back to the Western Zhou Dynasty (1122-771 B C) It is also known that translation started to boom in the Ming Dynasty, which was five hundred years ago.

In the past five hundred years, a large number of Chinese cultural works were translated into many languages of ASEAN countries and many of which have been integrated into their local cultures. China has also translated a lot of works of ASEAN countries. Translation is beneficial to inheritance and development of culture and upgrades the cultural exchanges between China and ASEAN to a higher level.

As Mr. Li Keqiang , Premier of the State Council of the People's Republic of China, pointed out in his speech at the opening ceremony of the 10th China-ASEAN Expo held in Nanning in September, 2013, China and ASEAN jointly created "10 golden years" of cooperation. And he called on both sides to upgrade their cooperation to a new level by creating "10 diamond years". In October, 2013, General Secretary Xi Jinping emphasized, in a meeting with Chinese diplomats, the importance of introducing China's domestic and foreign policies to other countries and regions, and making Chinese voice heard in the world. Xi also pointed out that "Chinese Dream" should be connected with her neighboring countries' dream of a better life and with the development prospect of those countries so as to build up a community of shared destiny. Against such a backdrop, it's of both historical and current significance to translate Chinese classics and introduce them to ASEAN countries.

Exchanges are reciprocal. According to *The Book of Rites*, behaviors that do not reciprocate are not consistent with rites. Like ASEAN countries, China has had excellent foreign cultural works translated and introduced domestically, and also translate and introduce to the outside world the essence of local culture and thoughts. Guangxi Normal University Press, one of the top presses in China that focus on enhancing the influence of the humanities, made the decision to publish *The Wisdom of the East Series*. It is not only a big event in Chinese academia, but also a necessary choice for China and ASEAN to communicate with each other and enhance mutual understanding. Guangdong University of Foreign Studies, and Guangxi University for Nationalities, the main undertakers of the translation project, are both national non-universal languages training bases for undergraduates and boast strengths of ASEAN languages. Cooperation between the two universities and the press will surely facilitate dissemination of traditional Chinese culture to ASEAN countries.

UNESCO officials hold the belief that cultural exchange is a new phenomenon of globalization.[1] We hope that our efforts could breathe the spirit of this historical momentum and help ASEAN countries understand Chinese culture better.

Liu Zhiqiang

January 25, 2015

---

[1] "Speech of Katerina stenou, Director of Division of Cultural Policies and Intercultural Dialogue", from *East Asia' s View on World Culture*. Beijing: Beijing University Press, 2004, p.3.

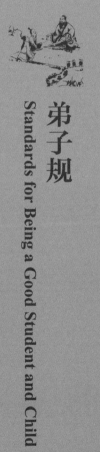

弟子规

Standards for Being a Good Student and Child

前言

中华文明历来重视儿童教育，有关儿童教育的文献也非常多，《弟子规》是其中的代表之一，它流传广泛，影响深远。

《弟子规》原本是中国学者李毓秀于清朝康熙年间（公元1662—1723年）编写的一本用于教育儿童的小册子，后经贾存仁于清朝乾隆年间（公元1736—1796年）修订，并命名为《弟子规》。它根据儒家经典《论语》的"学而"篇第六章"弟子入则孝，出则弟，谨而信，泛爱众，而亲仁。行有余力，则以学文"而阐发，全文只有1080个字，却包含了儒家提倡的孝、悌、忠、恕、礼、义、谨、信、爱众、亲仁、立志、勤学等重要思想，提出了许多为人处世的行为规范，是儒家思想启蒙教育的重要读本。

"弟子"有两个基本意思：一是指年幼的人，即少年儿童；二是指跟随老师读书学习的学生。"规"是指规范。"弟子规"就是子女或者儿童、学生应该明白的做人、做事的礼仪和规范。儿童时期，人的心智未成熟，容易受外界的影响，因此成长环境和学习内容在此时显得至关重要。《弟子规》引导孩子从小培养良好的生活习惯、优雅的举止和博爱的心胸，为人生奠定良好的基础。

《弟子规》形式上是三字一句、四句一韵，全文分为五个部分：总叙；入则孝，出则弟；谨而信；泛爱众，而亲仁；有余力，则学文。它文字浅显易懂，朗朗上口，说理简明具体，循循善诱，从清朝中晚期开始，就成为广泛流传的儿童启蒙读物。直到今天，《弟子规》仍然是许多中国父母和中小学选用的重要教育读物。儿童学习并背诵了《弟子规》，其中重要的道德观念、行为规范也就铭记于心了。

《弟子规》虽是童蒙读物，却有超越童蒙读物的普遍价值，不仅值得儿童读诵学习，也可供成人阅读体悟；不仅适合中国人学习，也可供世界各国人民观览。"不力行，但学文，长浮华，成何人；但力行，不学文，任己见，昧理真"体现一种文行并重、知行合一的认知世界的态度；"凡取与，贵分晓，与宜多，取宜少；将加人，先问己，己不欲，即速已"体现了互相尊重的人群相处之道；"能亲仁，无限好，德日进，过日少"体现了一种不断改造、发展自我的进取精神；"凡是人，皆须爱，天同覆，地同载"体现了平等、博爱的普世价值观。《弟子规》中的这些生活规范和礼仪在当今社会依然适用，所倡导的许多为人处世原则，可以作为人类共同的精神财富，代代相传。

中国文化重视家庭教育，重视伦理道德教育，与《弟子规》同类的古代童蒙教材还有《三字经》《百家姓》《千字文》，它们形式各有特点，内容各有侧重，共同构成了历史悠久、内容丰富的中国传统童蒙教育体系，都有在新时代传承学习的价值。

本书对《弟子规》全文进行了通俗易懂的释析，并配绘精美插图，期待这一人类教育智慧的经典能在当今时代得到更广泛的传播。

⁓ Foreword ⁓

Chinese have always attached great importance to education for children, and there're a host of books concerning child education. *Standards for Being a Good Student and Child* is one of the outstanding examples with widespread popularity and profound influence.

Standards for Being a Good Student and Child was written for child education by Li Yuxiu, a scholar in the reign of Emperor Kangxi of Qing Dynasty (1662-1723) and it was revised and renamed *Standards for Being a Good Student and Child* by Jia Cunren in the reign of Emperor Qianlong of Qing Dynasty (1736-1796). The book is based upon the Sixth Chapter of the Book Xue'er of the *Analects of Confucius* "Being dutiful to one's parents when at home and be respectful of one's elder brother when away from home. Being prudent and faithful, loving the general public and approaching the humane. If one has extra energy and time after accomplishing the above, one can devote himself to learning". A thin book with just 1080 Chinese characters as it is, the book contains important ideas including filial piety, respects for siblings, loyalty, reciprocity, rites, righteousness, prudence, faith, loving the general public, approaching the humane, having aspirations and assiduous study and it puts forward codes of conduct for people to establish themselves in the world, so it's an important Confucian book for enlightenment education.

Standards for Being a Good Student and Child is a book for students and children. It's about etiquette and norms that students and children should know. Children are not yet fully mature, and they are vulnerable to external influence, so a good growing environment and good books are important to them. *Standards for Being a Good Student and Child* teaches students and children to lay a solid foundation for their life by cultivating good lifestyle habits, good manners and a generous heart.

In the book, each sentence is composed of three Chinese characters and each four sentences are of the same rhyme. *Standards for Being a Good Student and Child* is divided into five parts: Preface, Filial Piety and Respects for Siblings, Prudence and Faith, Love the General Public and Approach the Humane, Devote to Learning with Extra Efforts. The book is easy to understand, catchy and good at giving systematic guidance. Thanks to such features, the book has become popular for enlightenment education since the middle of Qing Dynasty. After learning and memorizing the book, children will bear in mind the moral standards and codes of conduct.

Although it's a book for enlightenment education, *Standards for Being a Good Student and Child* is beyond a children's book. It's not only for children, but also for adults. It's not only for Chinese readers, but also for readers across the world. The saying that "Learning without practicing will make one superficially clever while practicing without learning will make one opinionated and unreasonable" reflects the attitude of perceiving the world by integrating theory with practice. The saying that "Giving and taking should be within the normal range and one should take less but give more. Ask yourself if you want the same thing to do unto you before doing it unto others. If you don't want, drop your idea immediately" reflects mutual respect in handling interpersonal relationships. The saying that "He who approaches the humane will benefit enormously as his virtues increase while errors decrease" reflects the attitude of unremitting self-improvement. The saying that "Love each other as we all live on the same planet with the same sky above us and the same soil beneath us "reflects the universal values of equality and philanthropy. The etiquette and codes of conduct mentioned in the book are applicable to today's world and can be passed down for generations as shared cultural and ethical wealth of human beings.

Chinese attach great importance to family education and ethical and moral education. *Standards for Being a Good Student and Child*, along with *Three-Character Classic, Hundred Family Surnames, and One Thousand Character Primer*, similar books for enlightenment education but with distinct features constitutes the long-established Chinese tradition of enlightenment education and is of current value.

The book is interpreted with easy-to-understand language and matched with beautiful illustrations. I hope the classic of education will be known by more people.

弟子规

总叙

弟子规　圣人训　首孝弟　次谨信
泛爱众　而亲仁　有余力　则学文

入则孝，出则弟

父母呼　应勿缓　父母命　行勿懒
父母教　须敬听　父母责　须顺承
冬则温　夏则凊　晨则省　昏则定
出必告　反必面　居有常　业无变
事虽小　勿擅为　苟擅为　子道亏
物虽小　勿私藏　苟私藏　亲心伤
亲所好　力为具　亲所恶　谨为去
身有伤　贻亲忧　德有伤　贻亲羞

亲爱我　孝何难　亲憎我　孝方贤
亲有过　谏使更　怡吾色　柔吾声
谏不入　悦复谏　号泣随　挞无怨
亲有疾　药先尝　昼夜侍　不离床
丧三年　常悲咽　居处变　酒肉绝
丧尽礼　祭尽诚　事死者　如事生
兄道友　弟道恭　兄弟睦　孝在中
财物轻　怨何生　言语忍　忿自泯
或饮食　或坐走　长者先　幼者后
长呼人　即代叫　人不在　己即到
称尊长　勿呼名　对尊长　勿见能
路遇长　疾趋揖　长无言　退恭立
骑下马　乘下车　过犹待　百步余
长者立　幼勿坐　长者坐　命乃坐
尊长前　声要低　低不闻　却非宜
进必趋　退必迟　问起对　视勿移
事诸父　如事父　事诸兄　如事兄

谨而信

朝起早　夜眠迟　老易至　惜此时
晨必盥　兼漱口　便溺回　辄净手
冠必正　纽必结　袜与履　俱紧切

弟子规
Standards for Being a Good Student and Child

置冠服　有定位　勿乱顿　致污秽
衣贵洁　不贵华　上循分　下称家
对饮食　勿拣择　食适可　勿过则
年方少　勿饮酒　饮酒醉　最为丑
步从容　立端正　揖深圆　拜恭敬
勿践阈　勿跛倚　勿箕踞　勿摇髀
缓揭帘　勿有声　宽转弯　勿触棱
执虚器　如执盈　入虚室　如有人
事勿忙　忙多错　勿畏难　勿轻略
斗闹场　绝勿近　邪僻事　绝勿问
将入门　问孰存　将上堂　声必扬
人问谁　对以名　吾与我　不分明
用人物　须明求　倘不问　即为偷
借人物　及时还　后有急　借不难
凡出言　信为先　诈与妄　奚可焉
话说多　不如少　惟其是　勿佞巧
奸巧语　秽污词　市井气　切戒之
见未真　勿轻言　知未的　勿轻传
事非宜　勿轻诺　苟轻诺　进退错
凡道字　重且舒　勿急疾　勿模糊
彼说长　此说短　不关己　莫闲管
见人善　即思齐　纵去远　以渐跻
见人恶　即内省　有则改　无加警

唯德学　唯才艺　不如人　当自砺
若衣服　若饮食　不如人　勿生戚
闻过怒　闻誉乐　损友来　益友却
闻誉恐　闻过欣　直谅士　渐相亲
无心非　名为错　有心非　名为恶
过能改　归于无　倘掩饰　增一辜

泛爱众，而亲仁

凡是人　皆须爱　天同覆　地同载
行高者　名自高　人所重　非貌高
才大者　望自大　人所服　非言大
己有能　勿自私　人所能　勿轻訾
勿谄富　勿骄贫　勿厌故　勿喜新
人不闲　勿事搅　人不安　勿话扰
人有短　切莫揭　人有私　切莫说
道人善　即是善　人知之　愈思勉
扬人恶　即是恶　疾之甚　祸且作
善相劝　德皆建　过不规　道两亏
凡取与　贵分晓　与宜多　取宜少
将加人　先问己　己不欲　即速已
恩欲报　怨欲忘　报怨短　报恩长
待婢仆　身贵端　虽贵端　慈而宽

势服人　心不然　理服人　方无言
同是人　类不齐　流俗众　仁者稀
果仁者　人多畏　言不讳　色不媚
能亲仁　无限好　德日进　过日少
不亲仁　无限害　小人进　百事坏

有余力，则学文

不力行　但学文　长浮华　成何人
但力行　不学文　任己见　昧理真
读书法　有三到　心眼口　信皆要
方读此　勿慕彼　此未终　彼勿起
宽为限　紧用功　工夫到　滞塞通
心有疑　随札记　就人问　求确义
房室清　墙壁净　几案洁　笔砚正
墨磨偏　心不端　字不敬　心先病
列典籍　有定处　读看毕　还原处
虽有急　卷束齐　有缺坏　就补之
非圣书　屏勿视　蔽聪明　坏心志
勿自暴　勿自弃　圣与贤　可驯致

总叙
Preface

【题解】

总叙部分首先说明《弟子规》的成文依据，并非作者杜撰，而是出自至圣先师孔子的遗训。接着引用《论语》里面孔子的一段话，简明扼要地概括了《弟子规》的内容，告诉人们教育子弟应谨遵圣人的教诲，以免误入歧途。

〔Explanatory Notes〕

The Preface first explains the basis of the book. It's not fabricated by the author, but is based upon the sayings of Confucius, the Extremely Sage Departed Teacher. Then, the Preface quotes a paragraph from the *Analects of Confucius* to briefly summarize the content of the book and asks people to follow the instructions of Confucius and avoid going astray.

1. 弟子规　圣人训　首孝弟　次谨信
泛爱众　而亲仁　有余力　则学文

【释文】

　　《弟子规》这本书，是依据至圣先师孔子的教诲而编成的。人首先要做到孝顺父母，友爱兄弟姊妹；其次言语行为要小心谨慎，讲诚信；要平等对待、关爱他人，亲近有仁德的人，向他们学习；这些事情做了之后，还有多余的时间、精力，就应该好好学习典籍，以获取有益的学问。

【Source】

　　Standards for Being a Good Student and Child is written based upon the instructions of Confucius, the Extremely Sage Departed Teacher. One should first be filial to one's parents and respectful of one's siblings. One should also be discreet in his words and deeds and be trustworthy. One should treat each other as equal and be friendly to others. One should approach the humane and learn from them. If one has extra efforts after accomplishing the above, one should devote himself to learning classics in order to obtain useful knowledge.

【解析】

孔子是儒家文化的创始人，他对中国文化的影响广泛而深远，被后世尊称为"至圣先师"。孔子的言论集中见于《论语》一书，《弟子规》就是根据《论语》当中孔子所说"弟子入则孝，出则弟，谨而信，泛爱众，而亲仁。行有余力，则以学文"一句而来的。孔子教育学生首重德行，德行方面，又首推孝悌。孝指善于侍奉父母，悌指善于侍奉兄长。家庭是构成社会的基本单位，教育应当从家庭开始。孝悌是人类共有的基本情感，是维系家庭稳定、延续的重要因素，孔子教育学生首重孝悌可谓意味深远。人随着年龄的增长，交际圈不断扩大，教育的内容、范围和深度也随之扩大，从家庭扩大到社会、国家，从家人扩大到朋友乃至陌生人。与人相处是一门大学问，值得每一个人深究。除了这门学问还有文献知识，文献象征历史的经验和智慧，是最便捷、最集中的前人的经验和智慧的学习平台，人们可以通过对文献典籍的学习，快速、高效地获得前人的经验、智慧，开阔视野，提升自己的生命境界。

【**Comments**】

Confucius was the founder of Confucianism. Owing to his enormous and profound influence upon Chinese culture, Confucius was honored as the Extremely Sage Departed Teacher. His sayings are mainly compiled in the *Analects of Confucius and the Standards for Being a Good Student and Child* is written based upon the saying in the *Analects of Confucius* "One should first be filial to one's parents and respectful of one's siblings. One should be discreet in his words and deeds and be trustworthy. One should treat each other as equal and be friendly to others. One should approach the humane and learn from them. If one has extra efforts after accomplishing the above, one should devote himself to learning classics in order to obtain useful knowledge". Confucius asked his disciples to value virtues and he pointed out that filial piety to one's parents and respects for one's siblings were the top virtues. The family is the basic unit of the society, so education should start from family. Filial piety and respects for one's siblings are the shared emotions of human beings and essential parts for stability and continuity of family. It's of deep significance for Confucius to teach his disciples to prioritize filial piety and respects for their siblings. As we get older, we expand our circles and embrace education and knowledge with scale, scope and intensity. Our education expands from our family to our society and our country; from our family members to our friends and even strangers. We should learn how to get along well with others and also we should learn about literature. Literature serves as the quickest and the most concentrated access to the wisdom and lessons of our ancestors. By learning literature, we will acquire the knowledge and wisdom of our ancestors in a quick and effective way, broaden our visions and improve our life state.

入则孝，出则弟

Filial Piety and Respects for Siblings

【题解】

　　"孝"是指儿女孝敬父母，"弟"是指敬爱兄弟姐妹。"入则孝，出则弟"，是说年轻人出入起居，在家出外，都要尊敬父母，友爱兄弟。

【Explanatory Notes】

Being filial to one's parents and being respectful of one's siblings.

2. 父母呼　应勿缓　父母命　行勿懒

【释文】

父母呼唤，不要慢吞吞很久才应答；父母交代的事情，要立刻动身去做，不可拖延或偷懒。

【Source】

When parents call their children, they should answer immediately. When parents ask their children to do something, they should do it quickly.

3. 父母教　须敬听　父母责　须顺承

【释文】

　　父母做教导，应当恭听；自己做错了事，父母责备，应当虚心接受。

【Source】

When parents instruct their children, they should listen with deference. When parents reproach their children for their wrongdoings, they should accept criticism with an open mind.

4. 冬则温 夏则清 晨则省 昏则定

【释文】

　　冬天要让父母的住所暖和，夏天要让父母住得凉爽。早晨起床之后，要去向父母问安；晚上要去看父母，让父母睡得安稳。

【Source】

　　Keep your parents warm in winter while keeping them cool in summer. Say hello to your parents after getting up in the morning while make sure your parents sleep well at night.

5. 出必告　反必面　居有常　业无变

【释文】

　　离家外出时，须告诉父母要到哪里去，回家后要当面禀报父母自己回来了。平时起居作息要有规律，从事的职业要保持稳定，不要任意改变。

【Source】

Tell your parents about your destinations before leaving home and see your parents and let them know you're back after returning home. Lead a regular life and have a steady job.

6. 事虽小　勿擅为　苟擅为　子道亏

【释文】
　　纵然是小事，也不要任性，擅自做主，而不向父母禀告。如果任性而为，出了错，就有损为人子女的本分。

【Source】

　　Do not make an arbitrary decision on even a small matter without letting your parents know. A wayward child will be easy to make mistakes and is not dutiful.

7. 物虽小　勿私藏　苟私藏　亲心伤

【释文】
　　不属于自己的东西，即使再小也不可以私自据为己有。如果私藏，品德就有了污点，父母知道了就会伤心。

【Source】
　　Do not take what is not yours as your own even if it is small. Otherwise, it'll be a taint on your honor and your parents will be heartbroken after they learn about what you've done.

8. 亲所好　力为具　亲所恶　谨为去

【释文】

　　父母所喜好的东西，应该尽力去准备；父母所厌恶的东西，要小心谨慎地去除（包括自己的坏习惯）。

【Source】

　　Do whatever your parents like and get rid of whatever they dislike, including your bad habits.

9. 身有伤　贻亲忧　德有伤　贻亲羞

【释文】

　　自己的身体若受到损伤，会给父母带来担忧；自己的品德有了污点，会给父母带来羞愧。

【Source】

　　Injuries to your body will worry your parents and your moral taints will disgrace them.

10. 亲爱我　孝何难　亲憎我　孝方贤

【释文】

当父母喜爱我们的时候，孝顺并不难；当父母厌恶我们，或者管教过于严厉的时候，我们一样孝顺，这才难能可贵。

【Source】

It's not difficult for us to be filial to our parents when we are their beloved whereas it is commendable if we remain filial to our parents when we are disliked by them or have a strict upbringing.

11. 亲有过　谏使更　怡吾色　柔吾声

【释文】

　　父母有了过失，子女应当小心劝其改正；劝的时候要和颜悦色，声音要轻柔平和。

【Source】

　　Sons and daughters should carefully advise their parents to correct their mistakes. Sons and daughters should advise their parents with a kind and pleasant countenance and soft voice.

12. 谏不入　悦复谏　号泣随　挞无怨

【释文】

　　如果父母不接受规劝，也不要着急，待父母情绪好时再劝；我们虽难过得痛哭流涕，也要恳求父母改过，纵然遭到责打，也无怨无悔，以免父母一错再错，铸成大错。

【Source】

　　If their parents do not accept their advice, sons and daughters should be patient and do not advice their parents until they are in good mood. To prevent their parents from making bigger mistakes, although they are grieved and shed bitter tears, sons and daughters should plead with their parents to correct their mistakes. Even if they are blamed and beaten, sons and daughters should bear no grudges.

13. 亲有疾　药先尝　昼夜侍　不离床

【释文】

　　父母生病时，喂他们吃药自己要先尝；他们病情严重时，要昼夜在床前服侍，不可以随便离开。

【Source】

　　Sons and daughters should taste the medicine before feeding their sick parents. They should wait on their parents day and night without leaving their bedside when their parents are seriously ill.

14. 丧三年　常悲咽　居处变　酒肉绝

【释文】

　　父母去世之后守孝三年，其间应常悲思、哭泣，感怀父母的恩德。这期间的生活起居也要有调整、改变，力求简朴，不喝酒、不吃肉。

【Source】

　　Sons and daughters should observe mourning for their deceased parents for three years and they should recall with deep sorrow and tears and show their gratitude for the love and care given by their parents to them since their childhood and do not drink alcohol or eat meat and lead a simple life during the three years of mourning.

15. 丧尽礼　祭尽诚　事死者　如事生

【释文】

办理父母的丧事要尽心，使之符合礼节，祭祀时要诚心诚意。对待已经去世的父母，要像他们在世时一样对他们保持恭敬。

【Source】

Sons and daughters should arrange funerals of their parents with all their hearts and make sure the funeral arrangement is in accordance with rites. They should earnestly offer sacrifices to their dead parents and serve them with the same reverence as if they were alive.

16. 兄道友　弟道恭　兄弟睦　孝在中

【释文】

　　兄姐对待弟妹要友爱，弟妹对待兄姐要恭敬。兄弟姐妹和睦相处，对父母的孝顺自然包含其中了。

【Source】

　　Elder sisters and brothers should love their younger siblings while younger sisters and brothers should respect their elder siblings. Siblings should live in harmony, which is a token of filial piety to their parents.

17. 财物轻　怨何生　言语忍　忿自泯

【释文】

　　看轻财物，不斤斤计较，怨恨就无从生起。说话相互尊重、忍让，隔阂怨恨自然就消失了。

【Source】

　　Treat material wealth lightly and do not be calculating, so there will be no grudges. Treat each other with respect and tolerance, so there will be no resentment.

18. 或饮食　或坐走　长者先　幼者后

【释文】

不论吃饭、喝水，还是就座、行走，都要长幼有序，让年长者在先，年幼者居后。

【Source】

The elder should be duly respected. Let the elder go first and the young follow them when eating, drinking, sitting and walking.

19. 长呼人　即代叫　人不在　己即到

【释文】

　　年长者呼唤他人时，自己听到了就代为呼叫；若所叫的人不在，自己就到年长者跟前听候吩咐。

【Source】

　　When an elder is asking for someone, get that person for him if you have heard it. If you cannot find the person, go to the elder's side and put yourself at the elder's service.

20. 称尊长　勿呼名　对尊长　勿见能

【释文】

　　称呼长辈，不可以直呼姓名。在尊长面前，要谦虚有礼，不要炫耀自己的才能。

【Source】

　　Do not address the elder disrespectfully by name. Be humble and polite and do not show off your talents in front of the elder.

21. 路遇长　疾趋揖　长无言　退恭立

【释文】

　　路上遇见长辈，应快步向前问好行礼，如果长辈没有说话，就恭敬退后站立一旁。

【Source】

　　When seeing an elder you know in the street, quickly walk forward and greet the elder. If the elder does not say a word, step back and stand aside reverently.

22. 骑下马 乘下车 过犹待 百步余

【释文】

　　骑马或乘车时，路上遇见长辈应下马或下车问候，等到长辈离去稍远，约百步之后，才可以上车或上马离开。

【Source】

　　When seeing an elder you know on a horse or in a carriage, get down from your horse or carriage and greet the elder. Do not get on the horse or carriage until the elder is about 100 paces away.

23. 长者立　幼勿坐　长者坐　命乃坐

【释文】

　　长辈站着，幼者不可以坐；长辈坐定以后，吩咐幼者坐下才可以坐。

【Source】

The young should not take seats while the elder are standing. The young should stand until the elder sit down and ask the young to do the same.

24. 尊长前　声要低　低不闻　却非宜

【释文】

　　与尊长交谈，声音要柔和适中，但声音太小以至让人听不清楚，就不恰当了。

【Source】

　　Speak softly when talking with the elder, but try not to be too low to be heard, which is not appropriate.

25. 进必趋　退必迟　问起对　视勿移

【释文】

　　有事要到尊长面前，应快步向前；退回去时，则应走慢一些。当长辈问话时，要站起来礼貌作答，不可以东张西望。

【Source】

　　If asked for by an elder, walk quickly towards him. When leaving, try not to walk hurriedly. Be polite and avoid looking around when answering questions of the elder.

26. 事诸父　如事父　事诸兄　如事兄

对待叔叔、伯伯等尊长，也要像对待自己的父亲一样；对待同族的兄长，也要像对待自己的亲兄长一样。

【Source】

Serve your uncles as if serving your father. Treat your cousins as if they were your own siblings.

【解析】

父母给予子女生命，爱护子女，竭尽心力为子女创造良好的成长环境而无怨无悔；孝敬父母，让父母安心，是子女报答父母恩德最直接的方式。孝的情感应伴随着人的一生，即使父母去世了，儿女适时地怀念也是孝的表现。同时，"孝"又不是一味地听从父母，作为子女若是发现父母有过失，子女应当以恰当方式规劝父母。

兄弟姐妹之间有血缘关系、手足之情，应该互相关爱、共同成长。年少者对待兄姐要恭敬，乃至对待所有年长于自己的都要怀有恭敬、尊重之心。反之，长辈、兄姐也要照顾、爱护晚辈或弟妹。家庭是社会的基本单位，人若能在家庭中培养、呵护孝悌的情感，将为发展其他美好品质打下基础，同时孝悌之情所培养起来的爱心也有可能延伸到家庭之外，惠及他人，这就是孟子所谓"老吾老，以及人之老；幼吾幼，以及人之幼"。

【 Comments 】

Our parents give birth to us and do their utmost to take good care of us and provide us with a good growing environment, so the most direct way for us to show our gratitude to them is to be dutiful to them and avoid worrying them. We should observe the filial piety throughout our whole life. It's also filial duty to remember our deceased parents. However, filial duty does not call for blind obedience to our parents. If our parents make mistakes, we should appropriately advise them to correct them.

Siblings are bonded by blood, and they should love each other and grow together. The younger siblings should respect the elder ones while the elder siblings should take care of the younger ones. The family is the basic unit of the society and if one is dutiful to one's parents, show respects for one's elder siblings and take care of one's younger siblings, one will have the solid foundation for developing other good qualities. In addition, a loving person will not only love his family members, but also others. Like what Mencius said, "Expand the respect for the aged in one's own family to those of other families; expand the love of the young in one's own family to those of other families".

谨而信

Prudence and Faith

【题解】

"谨"是指行为稳重、谨慎，在这里是指行为举止和衣服装束要端庄恭敬，不能随随便便。"信"是指诚实、守信，不虚言。这一部分围绕衣、食、住、行提出了许多规范和人际交往中应当遵守的一些原则，目的是让人养成良好的生活习惯和优雅得体的言行举止，提高个人德行和才能。

【Explanatory Notes】

Prudence refers to behaving properly and dressing appropriately. Faith refers to honesty, credibility and no falsehoods. Centering on clothing, food, shelter and transportation, this part puts forward norms and principles people should follow in handling interpersonal relationships with the purpose of helping young people to cultivate good lifestyle habits and decent manners and enhance their virtues.

27. 朝起早　夜眠迟　老易至　惜此时

【释文】

清晨要尽早起床，晚上要迟些才睡，人生短暂，少年不经意间就变成老年，要珍惜时间。

【Source】

Get up early in the morning and try not to get to bed too early at night. Life is so short that the young grow old even without noticing, so treasure time.

28. 晨必盥　兼漱口　便溺回　辄净手

【释文】

　　早晨起床后，务必洗脸、漱口。大小便后要洗手。

【Source】

　　Wash your face and brush your teeth after getting up in the morning and wash your hands after using the toilet.

29. 冠必正　纽必结　袜与履　俱紧切

【释文】

帽子要戴端正，衣服纽扣要扣好，袜子要穿整齐，鞋带要系紧。

【Source】

Wear your hat straight and button up your clothes. Wear your socks neatly and tie up your shoes.

30. 置冠服 有定位 勿乱顿 致污秽

【释文】

脱下来的衣服、帽子都要放在固定的位置，不要随手乱丢乱放，以免弄脏、弄皱。

【Source】

Put your clothes and hats in a fixed position and do not leave them all over the house in case of becoming dirty.

31. 衣贵洁　不贵华　上循分　下称家

【释文】

　　穿衣服注重整洁，不必讲究昂贵华丽，既应适合自己的身份及场合，也要符合家庭的经济状况。

【Source】

　　Neat and clean clothes outweigh splendid attire. Wear clothes that accord with your capacity and occasions as well as your financial status.

32. 对饮食　勿拣择　食适可　勿过则

【释文】

不要挑食、偏食；饮食要适可而止，不可吃得过饱。

【Source】

Do not be picky about food. Be temperate in eating and drinking and avoid overeating.

33. 年方少　勿饮酒　饮酒醉　最为丑

【释文】

青少年时期，不要饮酒；人一喝醉，丑态毕露，非常难看。

【Source】

Do not drink alcohol when young for if you get drunk, you will show the cloven hoof.

34. 步从容　立端正　揖深圆　拜恭敬

【释文】

　　走路时步伐应当从容稳重，站立的姿势要端正。问候他人行作揖礼要把身子深躬下去，行拜礼要毕恭毕敬。

【Source】

　　Walk steadily and stand straight. Bow deeply with reverence when greeting others.

35. 勿踐閾　勿跛倚　勿箕踞　勿搖髀

【释文】

　　进门时不要踩到门槛，不要用一条腿支撑身体斜着站立，坐下时不要随意伸开双腿像簸箕一样，不要摇晃大腿。

【Source】

　　Do not step on the threshold when entering a room. Do not stand on one leg. Do not have your legs sprawl out or shake them when seated.

36. 缓揭帘　勿有声　宽转弯　勿触棱

【释文】

　　进门时缓缓掀开门帘，不要发出很大声响。走路转弯时要把弯转得大些，以免触碰到物体的棱角而受伤。

【Source】

　　Gently lift the door curtain without making great noise when entering a room. When turning a corner, try to leave enough room in case of injuries caused by sharp edges of objects.

37. 执虚器　如执盈　入虚室　如有人

【释文】

　　拿着空的器具，也要像里面装满东西时一样小心。进入无人的房间，也要像有人在一样。

【Source】

Hold an empty container carefully as if it were full. Enter an empty room as if it were occupied.

38. 事勿忙　忙多错　勿畏难　勿轻略

【释文】

做事情不要匆匆忙忙，匆忙容易出错；不要怕困难，不要轻率随便、敷衍了事。

【Source】

Haste makes waste. Fear no difficulties and do not do things carelessly.

39. 斗闹场　绝勿近　邪僻事　绝勿问

【释文】

　　打架闹事的场所绝对不要接近；一些邪恶下流、荒诞不经的事，也不要好奇地去追问。

【Source】

Never approach those who are fighting. Never inquire about indecent things out of curiosity.

40. 将入门　问孰存　将上堂　声必扬

【释文】

　　要进入家门之前，应先问"有人在吗"，进入客厅之前，声音要高一些（让屋里的人知道有人来了）。

【Source】

Ask if there's someone inside before entering the main entrance. Raise your voice so that people inside will know you're coming before entering the living room.

41. 人问谁　对以名　吾与我　不分明

　　当有人问"你是谁"的时候，应该报出自己的名字，如果只是说"我，我"，对方就不知道你是谁。

【Source】

　　When asked about who you are, tell the person your name rather than "I" for the person will not know who you are with that reply.

42. 用人物　须明求　倘不问　即为偷

【释文】

　　要用别人的东西，必须公开向物主请求；假如不经过别人的允许就拿，那就是偷窃了。

【Source】

　　Ask the owner for permission before using what belongs to the owner. Otherwise, it's stealing.

43. 借人物　及时还　后有急　借不难

【释文】
　　借来的物品，要及时归还，日后有急用时，再去借用就不难。

【Source】
　　Return duly what you've borrowed, so it won't be difficult for you to borrow it again in case of urgent need.

44. 凡出言　信为先　诈与妄　奚可焉

【释文】

开口说话，诚信为先；欺骗或花言巧语怎么可以呢?

【Source】

Honesty should be put first when talking. He who says deceiving words is not trustworthy.

45. 话说多　不如少　惟其是　勿佞巧

【释文】

话多不如话少，实事求是就好，不可花言巧语。

【Source】

Speaking less is better than speaking more. Speak the truth and avoid falsehoods.

46. 奸巧语　秽污词　市井气　切戒之

【释文】

　　虚伪奸诈的语言，下流肮脏的话，以及街头无赖粗俗的习气，务必要戒除。

【Source】

　　Get rid of deceptive and foul language together with vulgar habits.

47. 见未真　勿轻言　知未的　勿轻传

【释文】

　　没有看真切的事情，不要轻易发表意见；没有了解准确的事，不要轻易传播散布。

【Source】

　　Do not express your opinions on what you have not seen clearly. Do not spread the news if you are uncertain of its accuracy.

48. 事非宜　勿轻诺　苟轻诺　进退错

【释文】

　　事情不妥当，不能轻易允诺别人，如果不经思考便允诺别人，就会进退两难。

【Source】

　　Do not make promises about inappropriate things. You will put yourself in dilemma if you make a rash promise.

49. 凡道字　重且舒　勿急疾　勿模糊

【释文】

　　讲话时应当言语持重、语气舒缓，不要说得太快，也不要含糊不清。

【Source】

　　When speaking, make sure your words are clear, your speed is not fast and your voice not slurred.

50. 彼说长　此说短　不关己　莫闲管

【释文】

他人评论人事的是非好坏，与自己无关，不要去参与。

【Source】

Some people like to comment on others. It's none of your business and do not engage yourself in it.

51. 见人善　即思齐　纵去远　以渐跻

【释文】

　　看见他人有优点，自己也要努力做到，即使相差很远，只要坚持不懈也能逐渐赶上。

【Source】

　　On seeing a man of virtue, try to become his equal. Even if you are a far cry from the person, given enough perseverance, you will still be able to keep pace with him.

52. 见人恶　即内省　有则改　无加警

【释文】

　　看见别人的缺点，要反躬自省，如果自己也有这些缺点，就要及时改正，如果没有，就要保持警醒，远离这些缺点。

【Source】

　　Examine yourself when noticing shortcomings of others and eliminate them if you have the same and keep yourself away from them if you don't have them.

53. 唯德学　唯才艺　不如人　当自砺

【释文】

　　自己的品德、学问和才能技艺，如果有不如人的地方，应当自我激励，奋发图强。

【Source】

　　Inspire yourself to work harder if you are inferior to others in morality, knowledge and skills.

54. 若衣服　若饮食　不如人　勿生戚

【释文】
穿着、饮食不如他人，不要忧伤、自卑。

【Source】
Do not feel sad or self-abased when you are inferior to others in clothing and food.

55. 闻过怒　闻誉乐　损友来　益友却

【释文】

　　听到别人指出自己的缺点就生气，听到别人称赞自己就高兴，那么有害的朋友就会集聚在身边，有益的朋友就会疏远。

【Source】

He who feels angry when his shortcomings are pointed out but joyful when receiving praise will be approached by bad friends and estranged from good friends.

56. 闻誉恐　闻过欣　直谅士　渐相亲

【释文】

　　听见别人的赞誉会感到不安，听见别人指出自己的缺点便十分欣喜，这样正直诚信的人就会越来越乐于和自己亲近。

【Source】

He who feels uneasy when receiving praise but delighted when being pointed out his shortcomings will be approached by more and more men of integrity.

57. 无心非　名为错　有心非　名为恶

【释文】

无意之间犯的错误称为过错，若是有意犯错那就是罪恶了。

【Source】

A mistake made unintentionally is only an error whereas a mistake made by design is evil.

58. 过能改　归于无　倘掩饰　增一辜

【释文】

犯了过错勇于改正，错误就可以消除；犯了错误还要加以掩饰，那就是错上加错了。

【Source】

Mistakes are no longer mistakes when corrected whereas they become serious mistakes if they are glossed over.

【解析】

良好的行为习惯让人受益一生，同时也能带给他人便利。儒家把"信"与"仁、义、礼、智"并列为五种伦常（美德），可见其重要，它是为人处事必须遵守的重要原则。

【Comments】

Good lifestyle habits will benefit us throughout our whole life and bring convenience to others. Confucianism puts faith on a par with humaneness, righteousness, rites and wisdom as one of the five virtues, which shows the importance of faith. It is a crucial principle for us to follow in handling interpersonal relationships.

弟子规
Standards for Being a Good Student and Child

泛爱众，而亲仁

Love the General Public and Approach the Humane

【题解】

"泛爱众"，是指平等地对待、友爱一切人。"亲仁"指亲近有仁德的人，以及一切品行出众的人。这两者并不矛盾，人因为成长环境、学习条件及个人努力程度的不一样，能力有高低，品德有高下，"亲仁"就是鼓励人主动向优秀的人物学习，不断提高自己的品行。

【 Explanatory Notes 】

Loving the general public refers to treating others as equals and loving them all while approaching the humane refers to approaching those with virtues, which are two sides of a coin. Disparities in growing environment, learning conditions and individual efforts lead to distinct abilities and morality, so approaching the humane encourages people to take the initiative to learn from those with virtues and continuously enhance their own virtues.

59. 凡是人　皆须爱　天同覆　地同载

【释文】

　　只要是人，都要关心爱护，人们头顶的是同一片蓝天，脚踏的是同一片土地。

【Source】

Love each other as we all live on the same planet with the same sky above us and the same soil beneath us.

60. 行高者　名自高　人所重　非貌高

【释文】

　　品德高尚的人，名声自然高远。人们所看重的不是相貌出众。

【Source】

Those with virtues will surely enjoy a high reputation. What people value are not good looks.

61. 才大者　望自大　人所服　非言大

【释文】

才学深厚的人，声望自然会高。人们所佩服的并不是话语浮夸。

【Source】

Those with immense erudition will surely enjoy a high reputation.
What people admire is not bombastic language.

62. 己有能　勿自私　人所能　勿轻訾

【释文】

　　自己有能力就不要自私自利；他人有能力，不要轻视、说人坏话。

【Source】

　　A man of ability should not be selfish. Do not despise or speak ill of men of ability.

63. 勿谄富　勿骄贫　勿厌故　勿喜新

【释文】

不要去讨好巴结富人，不要在穷人面前炫耀自夸；对任何事物都不要喜新厌旧，疏远故人，抛弃优良传统。

【Source】

Do not curry favor with the rich and do not show off wealth in front of the poor. Do not reject the old and crave for the new. Do not alienate yourself from old friends and do not abandon fine traditions.

64. 人不闲　勿事搅　人不安　勿话扰

【释文】

　　别人正在忙碌，不要拿小事去打搅他；别人身心欠安时，不要用闲话去打搅他。

【Source】

Do not bother the person who is busy with trivial matters and do not bother the person who is ill with small talk.

65. 人有短　切莫揭　人有私　切莫说

【释文】

　　别人的缺点，千万不要去恶意揭露；别人的隐私，切记不要去张扬。

【Source】

Never expose others' defects out of malice and never disclose others' secrets.

66. 道人善　即是善　人知之　愈思勉

【释文】

赞美他人的善行就是行善。他人听到称赞之后，必定会更加勤勉行善。

【Source】

It's a good deed to sing highly of good deeds done by others. On hearing praise, others will work harder to do more good deeds.

67. 扬人恶　即是恶　疾之甚　祸且作

【释文】

张扬他人的过失就是犯错。批评太过分了，可能会带来新的灾祸。

【Source】

It's a fault to disclose others' mistakes, and excessively criticizing others for their mistakes will cross the line and invite trouble.

68. 善相劝　德皆建　过不规　道两亏

【释文】

　　朋友之间互相规过劝善，良好的品德就能建立。如果有错不互相规劝，双方品德都会受损害。

【Source】

　　Friends should advise each other to do good deeds while avoiding bad deeds, thus their virtues are cultivated; otherwise, their virtues will be damaged.

69. 凡取与　贵分晓　与宜多　取宜少

【释文】

　　索取与付出，贵在有分寸，付出的要多，索取的要少。

【Source】

Giving and taking should be within the normal range. One should take less but give more.

70. 将加人　先问己　己不欲　即速已

　　即将对他人做某事时，先要反省问问自己愿不愿意被这样对待，如果自己不愿意，就要立刻停止这样做。

【Source】

Ask yourself if you want the same thing to do unto you before doing it unto others. If you don't want, drop your idea immediately.

71. 恩欲报　怨欲忘　报怨短　报恩长

【释文】

　　受人恩惠要时时想着报答，别人有对不起自己的事，应该宽大为怀尽快把它忘掉；对别人怨恨的时间越短越好，对别人报恩的时间越长越好。

【Source】

Always remember to repay others for their kindness to you and forget as soon as possible the bad things others have done to you. The sooner you leave behind grudges against others, the better. The longer you remember the kindness of others, the better.

72. 待婢仆 身贵端 虽贵端 慈而宽

【释文】

　　和家中的婢女与仆人相处，贵在自身行为端正；虽然贵在端正自身，但对待婢女与仆人时应当仁慈、宽容。

【Source】

　　When treating servants, behave properly, but with kindness and leniency.

73. 势服人　心不然　理服人　方无言

【释文】
　　用势力压服人，对方难免口服心不服；用道理说服别人，对方才会心悦诚服，没有怨言。

【Source】
　　People will pretend to be convinced if overwhelmed by your power whereas they will be completely convinced by reasoning.

74. 同是人　类不齐　流俗众　仁者稀

【释文】

　　同样是人，但人与人不一样，善恶邪正、心智高低不齐。普通的俗人多，品德高尚、仁慈宽厚的人少。

【Source】

Not all men are alike. The number of ordinary people surpasses that of people of high morality.

75. 果仁者　人多畏　言不讳　色不媚

【释文】

　　果真是仁者，大家都会敬畏他，他说话直言不讳、公正无私，不讨好他人。

【Source】

　　People are in awe of the humane for they are impartial, talk straight and do not fawn on others.

76. 能亲仁　无限好　德日进　过日少

【释文】

　　能够亲近有仁德的人，会有无限的好处，自己的德行会一天天进步，过失会一天天减少。

【Source】

He who approaches the humane will benefit enormously as his virtues increase while errors decrease.

77. 不亲仁　无限害　小人进　百事坏

【释文】

　　不肯亲近有仁德的人，会有无限的害处，小人会乘虚而入，很多事情会因此失败。

【Source】

　　He who refuses to approach the humane will inflict harm and will be doomed to failure in a lot of things as he associates with men without virtue.

【解析】

人类生活在同一片天空下，应当相互尊重，相互扶持，共同发展。这一部分把对亲人对朋友的爱扩展到对天下人的爱，旨在培养人广博的心胸和慈悲的情怀。泛爱众并非大而空的话，要求人必须掌握人际交往过程中的一些基本原则，从日常生活的细微处着手。

【 Comments 】

We live under the same sky, so we should respect each other and support each other for common development. This part expands the love for our family members and friends to all human beings, intending to cultivate broad mind and compassion. Loving the general public is not empty talk. It requires us to master basic principles of handling interpersonal relationships and begin with trivial mathers in our daily life.

弟子规
Standards for Being a Good Student and Child

有余力，则学文

Devote to Learning with Extra Efforts

【题解】

"有余力，则学文"，是说人在明白了基本的道德伦理和生活规范并能付诸实践后，就可以学习前人留下的各种文献了。人们可以通过学习文献知识，获取更广泛的知识，开阔视野，提升自己的文化涵养和精神境界。

【Explanatory Notes】

Devoting to learning with extra efforts means that one can learn works of literature after one has understood the basic ethics and moral standards and rules of social life and put what one has learnt into practice. One will accquire extensive knowledge and broaden one's vision and improve one's cultural literacy and achieve a higher level of thinking through reading works of literature.

78. 不力行　但学文　长浮华　成何人

【释文】

如果不注重实践，一味死读书，纵然有些知识，也只是增长自己浮华不实的习气，变成一个不切实际的人，如此读书又有何用？

【Source】

Learning without practicing will make one superficially clever. What's the use of learning without practicing?

79. 但力行　不学文　任己见　昧理真

【释文】

　　如果只是一味地卖力去做，不肯读书学习，就容易依着自己的偏见做事而不明真理。

【Source】

Practicing without learning will make one opinionated and unreasonable.

80. 读书法　有三到　心眼口　信皆要

【释文】

　　读书的方法注重三到——眼到、口到、心到，三者缺一不可，都很重要。

【Source】

Three things are essential in learning: use your eyes to see characters, use your mouth to read aloud and use your mind to think.

81. 方读此　勿慕彼　此未终　彼勿起

【释文】

　　正在读这本书，就不要想着别的书；这本书没读完，就不要开始读别的书。

【Source】

Focus on the book you are reading and do not start reading another one before finishing it.

82. 宽为限　紧用功　工夫到　滞塞通

【释文】

制定计划在时间上可以适当宽松一些，落实计划时，就要严格执行。日积月累，认识不断加深，原先困顿疑惑的地方自然明白了。

【Source】

Flexibility in making plans is allowable while strict implementation should be ensured. With time passing by, you will have a better understanding of what you have learnt and your puzzles will be solved.

83. 心有疑　随札记　就人问　求确义

【释文】

　　心中有疑问，应随时用笔记下来，一有机会立即向别人请教，以求了解其确切的意义。

【Source】

　　If you have a question, write it down immediately and grasp any chance to consult others about the answer.

84. 房室清　墙壁净　几案洁　笔砚正

【释文】

房间清洁，墙壁干净，书案整洁，笔墨纸砚放置整齐。

【Source】

Keep your room tidy and your walls clean. Keep your desk neat and put your writing brushes, paper, ink stick and ink stone in order.

85. 墨磨偏　心不端　字不敬　心先病

【释文】

　　写毛笔字前磨墨把墨条磨歪了，说明精神不集中；写出来的字如果歪斜了，说明心神不定。

【Source】

　　You are not focused if you rub your ink stick askew before writing. You have no peace of mind if your characters are written askew.

86. 列典籍　有定处　读看毕　还原处

【释文】

摆放书本要有固定的位置，读完要放回原处。

【Source】

Put your books in the fixed position and place them where they were after reading.

87. 虽有急　卷束齐　有缺坏　就补之

【释文】

读书时有急事要走开，要把书本收好。发现书有破损的地方，应及时修补好。

【Source】

Put away the book you are reading before attending to urgent business. Mend your torn books promptly.

88. 非圣书 屏勿视 蔽聪明 坏心志

【释文】

　　不是圣贤之书及有益身心健康的书籍，应该摒弃不看，因为邪僻的书会蒙蔽人的聪慧，败坏人的意志。

【Source】

　　Read only books of sages and that are beneficial to your health and mind for other books will mislead you and drain your will.

89. 勿自暴　勿自弃　圣与贤　可驯致

【释文】

不要轻视圣贤的教诲，不要放弃成为圣贤的努力，圣贤的境界虽高，但是只要按部就班、循序渐进去努力，是可以不断接近的。

【Source】

Never despise instructions of sages. Never give up emulating sages. You will approach them with consistent efforts.

【解析】

从古到今的文献知识浩如烟海，如果不遵守一些基本的学习方法和技巧，学习的效果会不甚理想，而一旦掌握了这些基本方法和技巧，就能取得事半功倍的效用。在学习的过程中，还要注重立下高远的志向，向古时候的圣贤们学习、看齐。

【 Comments 】

Works of literature from the past to the present are as plentiful as blackberries, so one can never learn them all efficiently unless employing some basic learning methods. Meanwhile, one should nurture a high ambition by emulating the sages.